Pebble® Plus

Investigate the Seasons
Let's Look at Spring

by Sarah L. Schuette

Consulting Editor: Gail Saunders-Smith, PhD

Capstone press®

Mankato, Minnesota

Pebble Plus is published by Capstone Press,
151 Good Counsel Drive, P.O. Box 669, Mankato, Minnesota 56002.
www.capstonepress.com

1 2 3 4 5 6 12 11 10 09 08 07

Library of Congress Cataloging-in-Publication Data
Schuette, Sarah L., 1976–
    Let's look at spring / by Sarah L. Schuette.
    p. cm.—(Pebble plus. Investigate the seasons)
    Summary: "Simple text and photographs present what happens to the weather, animals, and plants in
spring"—Provided by publisher.
    Includes bibliographical references and index.
    ISBN-13: 978-0-7368-6707-8 (hardcover)
    ISBN-10: 0-7368-6707-4 (hardcover)
    1. Animal behavior—Juvenile literature. 2. Spring—Juvenile literature. I. Title. II. Series.
QL753.S382 2007
508.2—dc22   2006020451

Editorial Credits
Martha E. H. Rustad, editor; Bobbi Wyss, set designer; Veronica Bianchini, book designer; Kara Birr,
    photo researcher; Scott Thoms, photo editor

Photo Credits
BigStockPhoto.com/George Muresan, 5
Corbis/Donna Disario, cover (background tree); Gabe Palmer, 20–21
Getty Images Inc./Stone/Andy Sacks, 10–11; The Image Bank/Harald Sund, 14–15
Peter Arnold/Hartmut Noeller, 6–7
Shutterstock/bora ucak, cover, 1 (magnifying glass); Clive Watkins, 1 (flowers); Danger Jacobs, cover (inset
    leaf); Radomir JIRSAK, 13; Shironina Lidiya Alexandrovna, 9
SuperStock/age fotostock, 19
UNICORN Stock Photos/Les Van, 17

The author dedicates this book to her friends Art and Barb Straub of Le Sueur, Minnesota.

Note to Parents and Teachers

The Investigate the Seasons set supports national science standards related to weather
and climate. This book describes and illustrates spring. The images support early readers
in understanding the text. The repetition of words and phrases helps early readers learn
new words. This book also introduces early readers to subject-specific vocabulary words,
which are defined in the Glossary section. Early readers may need assistance to read
some words and to use the Table of Contents, Glossary, Read More, Internet Sites, and
Index sections of the book.

Table of Contents

It's Spring!

How do you know

it's spring?

Spring is full of life.

5

Bright sunlight shines.

The next day rain falls.

Spring days are warmer

and wetter than winter days.

Sun and rain help
plants grow.
Everything is green again.

9

Animals in Spring

What happens

to animals in spring?

Robins feed their young

in nests.

Sheep graze

in green pastures.

Newborn lambs walk

on wobbly legs.

Plants in Spring

What happens

to plants in spring?

Tulips bloom.

Grass grows.

Blossoms cover cherry trees.

Bees buzz in and out

of the flowers.

Planting begins on farms.

Rows of crops

sprout in fields.

What's Next?

The weather gets warmer.

Spring is over.

What season comes next?

Glossary

blossom—a flower on a fruit tree or other plant

crop—a plant grown in large amounts; corn, wheat, soybeans, and oats are some crops planted in spring.

graze—to eat grass that is growing in a field

pasture—a field of grass where animals graze

season—one of the four parts of the year; winter, spring, summer, and fall are seasons.

sprout—to start to grow

wobbly—unsteady

Read More

Davis, Rebecca Fjelland. *Flowers and Showers: A Spring Counting Book.* Counting Books. Mankato, Minn.: Capstone Press, 2006.

Kalz, Jill. *Spring.* My First Look at Seasons. Mankato, Minn.: Creative Education, 2006.

Orme, Helen. *Why Do Plants Grow in Spring?* What? Where? Why? Milwaukee: Gareth Stevens, 2004.

Internet Sites

FactHound offers a safe, fun way to find Internet sites related to this book. All of the sites on FactHound have been researched by our staff.

Here's how:

1. Visit *www.facthound.com*

2. Choose your grade level.

3. Type in this book ID **0736867074** for age-appropriate sites. You may also browse subjects by clicking on letters, or by clicking on pictures and words.

4. Click on the **Fetch It** button.

FactHound will fetch the best sites for you!

Index

Word Count: 104
Grade: 1
Early-Intervention Level: 13